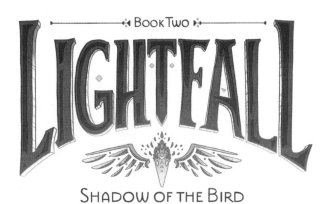

◄ Book Two ►

LIGHTFALL

SHADOW OF THE BIRD

You know, Hobbes, some days even my
lucky rocketship underpants don't help.

—Bill Watterson

BOOK TWO

LIGHTFALL

SHADOW OF THE BIRD

TIM PROBERT

HARPER
alley

An Imprint of HarperCollins Publishers

One more story. Which would you like to hear?

Hm.

Tell me about the Bird and the Sun.

Oh ho, again? Okay then.

Long ago there was a sun hovering above Irpa, high in the sky, making everything warm and bright.

Things were peaceful, but then something appeared. A bird—Kest Ke Belenus.

Kest was jealous of the love people had for the sun.

So he devoured it, plunging the entire world into empty darkness.

But the heroic Galdurians rose up and defeated Kest.

They rescued the sun's Flame from him and created the Lights that hover above Irpa today.

What if the Bird comes back?

Well, that would be very bad! But don't worry, little bumblebee, your ol' gramps won't let that happen.

Besides, you've got your magic lantern, so you'll never be in the dark . . .

Isn't that right, Bea?

I could see myself settling down in a place like this one day when I'm gray and wrinkled.

You are gray.

It **is** beautiful here.

I'd love to stay, but we have to find Gramps.

Or I do anyway.

You're right! What's our next move?

Everything's gone sideways. The Feather Knights took the Jar, which Kipp said is actually a piece of the sun—which is **insane**—and we still don't know where Gramps is or even where to start.

Here.

Hi there, friend.

You're here! I saw you in Lealand.

POP!

You made that lightning. You saved us.

Didn't make. Asked the storm for help.

I missed it. I was unconscious.

This way.

Shall we?

The Restless Sleeper has awoken.

The Restless Sleeper is Kest, right? The Bird?

Yes. It has the Flame. Its power grows. The Bird goes to Lealand and will take the Flame within the Light. Then the Flames within all the Lights.

How do you know this?

It has been seen and told by Irpa.

Irpa?
Like the
planet?

Yes.

You talk
to it?

Yes.

How?

This . . .

. . . is a bone
of Irpa.

Wow.
Okay, I **really** want
to know more
about that.

Sure, but let's stay on topic.

What is that
flame in the Jar?
Why does Kest
want it?

It is from the sun first.
Then from the fallen Light.

So Kipp
was telling
the truth.

Darkness will soon befall the Sea of Light.

No it won't. I will stop Kest.

No.

Oh, **yes** I will! The Galdurians defeated him once. I'll do it again.

There is a message from the wizard.

GRAMPS?! Is he here?!

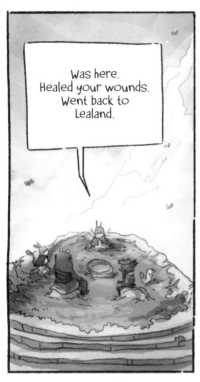

Was here.
Healed your wounds.
Went back to
Lealand.

Went back...
Without me?
Why?

The wizard asks you
to complete his quest.

Dear Beatrice,

I'm sorry to keep leaving you notes, but I couldn't wait for you to wake. There's too much to tell you here, so I will keep it short.

Watching over the Restless Sleeper was my task and I failed. The Jar of Endless Flame is on its way to him, and his power will grow once he has it.

I'm going to Lealand to warn the mara and evacuate the city before Kest arrives.

You must NOT follow me. Seriously this time.

Kest is too powerful for us to stop. My plan was to find Lorgon, the Lord of Waters, and ask for his help. My research says his realm is underground along the Lost River. You must be lost to find the river, then follow the fireflies once you are there. If anyone will know what to do, I believe it is Lorgon. Call it a hunch.

I need you to do this for me. Find Lorgon for the sake of us all.

Promise to see you again.

Love,
Gramps

PS- Say hello to the Galdurian for me!
He seems oddly familiar.

Lorgon . . . like the Spirit?
As in, one of the ancient beings
that created all of Irpa?

Yes.

How?!
Nobody's ever seen
a Spirit. And we're supposed
to find one and ask it for help?!
They might not be around
anymore. Or they might
not even be real!

They said the same thing about
Galdurians, to be fair. But even still,
I don't think searching for Lorgon
is the answer.

We **know** Kest is going to Lealand, so that's where **we** should go. The help of a Spirit is well and good, but we can stop this here and now.

?

Bea, are you coming?

It's okay if you stay, but I've made up my mind.

I'm gonna go to Lealand.

I... I—

I need some air!!

Air?

We're outside.

But does it even matter anyway? Gramps might be in danger.

Though what could I possibly do to help him?

Maybe that's just an excuse not to go back there.

I just want to find Gramps.

I want to go home.

I want this all to go away.

I want to disappear.

I want to start over.

You think I'm a coward, don't you, Nimm?

MRROWRR

Hey!

You're right. Lealand is in danger and so is Gramps. That's where we should go.

All right, Lealand! Reinforcements are on the way!

Once we get Gramps we can figure out all this Lorgon stuff.

Thank you for your generosity and hospitality, little friends.

Yeah. I'm Cad, this is Bea. That's Nimm. We never got your name.

Don't have names. Not really.

Well, that won't do. You want one?

SCHWWIPP

Ralph. Lizard. Crow. Grass. Dig, Cad Jr., Gil, Mouse, Fern—

Is there something you really like? You could go with that.

Perhaps.

Not really. Will think about it.

Take your time!

What do you think they'll call **me**?

:MRP:

25

What do you mean?

After I slay Kest! I'll be the greatest hero of the age. I'll need some catchy name for all the songs and things.

Like Cad the Great?

Yeah, but more exciting than that. Cadwallader the Conqueror!

That's a mouthful.

Yeah, and the tone isn't quite right. But I like the alliteration.

Cad the Courageous.

I like that!

Or how about—

?!

28

How . . . ?

Kest.

He just . . .
He didn't . . .

Somehow . . .

He did.

Gramps.

SoB
SoB

Cad, the world's going to end.

NO! No, it's not.

Kest won't leave that city.

Mark my words.

I'm with you . . .

Till the very end.

What **was** that?

A shadow of a thing.

Pure darkness.

These used to hunt us. After the sun, before the Lights. But this one won't be hunting any time soon.

Uh—Cad? Look!

SHKLOOOOOP!!

SKREEEE

RUN!!

THWUMP!

BUNGA?!

Make yerselfs useful— stab the glowy bit!!

For now, at least.

What are you and the Galdurian doing here? Didn't you get my note?

That was very brave. But you shouldn't be here! We're holding the gate while the last of the survivors clear out— You need to go too!

I'm sorry. We thought we could help.

Mr. Wizard. I—I can't believe it's you. I'm sorry, but I'm going after Kest.

Madness!!

Look at what he did! His power is unimaginable.

You can't defeat him on your own. You need **help**.

There isn't time! I won't let him destroy another Light!

Bea, we found your grandfather. You should go with him.

What are you doing?!

I told you—

I'm with you till the end.

That bird doesn't stand a chance.

SKREEE!!

SKLASHHHH

HNGH!

UNGH!

Look, Bea!

GO.

It's . . . warm?

We're near the heart of the Light.

There it is up ahead.

He's here.

STOP!!

KAA-SHOOM!!

We're too late.
We have to go.

We need help.
We **have** to find Lorgon.

BIRD!

WAIT!

GOTCHA!!

HNH!!

Are you okay?!

Maybe.

Are we dead?

WHAT?!

No.

I mean, I don't **think** so.

Look out for the water!

UHNF!

You almost rolled right in there.

SPLOSH

SPLUSH

You don't look so good.

Are you all right?

It's nothing. It's just . . . It's just really cold in here.

I hope everyone got away safely.

They've got your grandfather and Bunga watching their backs. They'll be fine.

Yeah.

But Kest has **another** Flame.

He's unstoppable.

We'll have none of that defeatist talk! **Nothing** is impossible. We just need a new plan.

So, what should that plan be?

Lorgon.

Oh right! Your grandfather's quest. Find a Spirit to fight a demon. Let's do it.

Demon . . .

Bea . . . Are you sure you're just cold?

A lot has happened. It's okay if you need to take a moment.

No.

No more wasting time. I'm fine.

Fair enough! First step, we find the Lost River.

I think this is it.

What?!

Gramps said it's underground, and you have to be lost to find it. We're underground and very lost. And this **is** a river.

It's just a gut feeling, really.

Maybe our Arsai friend sent us here.

That little guy is full of surprises.

YEEK!

Listen! Do you hear that?

Oh ho, I do!

Finally, some good luck.

They're riders!

We held the city as best we could. But there was no chance.

With our Light gone, shadowy creatures chased us down.

They only stopped when we reached the edge of your Light.

But we must not linger! The Bird will surely come here next.

The Bird . . .

Here.

Snore!!

BOISENBERRY & SNORE'S EXOTIC FRUIT EMPORIUM

This new business will never take off if you continue to eat the product!

I didn't! At least, I don't think I did.

He he he

The mara has returned!

Impossible!!

Absurd
nonsense!

It's absolute
rubbish!

Regretfully, it is
all true, as much as
it pains me to say.

Kest Ke Belenus has awoken.

The Bird is a **myth**! And even if he **was** real, legend says that he was destroyed hundreds of years ago.

Defeated, but not **destroyed**. And then put into a magical slumber.

Why spare such a creature?

I do not know.

How did he awaken?

I do not know that either. But it does not matter. All that matters is that he is now awake and wants to destroy every Light of Irpa.

Heh Heh
Heh Heh

Tell us, Pig Wizard . . . How is it that you know so much about this bird?

Because I'm the one who found him.

In my youth, I set out on a quest to find a way to revive the sun.

My first discovery was the Lost Flame from the Light of Tarian. A critical step in the right direction . . .

But my next discovery changed everything.

I found Kest, asleep in a crystal cage.

I realized that reviving the sun would mean nothing if Kest were to escape.

So I appointed myself as guardian of both the Flame and the slumbering bird.

Where is the Flame of Tarian now?

Kest has it. It surely gave him the strength to destroy the Light of Lealand.

Sounds like you didn't do a very good job at **either** of your tasks.

I didn't.

I am an old fool who has made many mistakes.

Mara, are we supposed to believe such wild words from this stranger?!

Pardon me, sir. But you **should**.

You **all** should. I saw the Bird take down our Light right before my eyes.

Lealand's mara chose not to listen, and now he's **gone**. Crushed under our broken light, and our city overtaken by shadows.

Well, that's no good.

Alfirid was a friend of my father's. He is not a stranger.

My father trusted his counsel and I will too.

Alfirid, what would you suggest we do?

My plan was to request the help of the Spirit Lorgon.

But my granddaughter and her friend, a Galdurian, are going in my stead.

Spirits and Galdurians! Praise Irpa, the pig is mad!

We need to find the **true cause** of what's happening!

We can't sit around waiting for some imaginary friend to save us!

Hello.

I didn't take anything, I swear!

Strange.

GAH!!

Where'd you come from?!

Wait, I know you. I saw you in Lealand.

You're friends with the frog and the girl.

Friends?
Yes, perhaps.

But you—
Whatever, it doesn't matter.

Where are they?

Unsure.

Fancy that.

Welp.

Good seeing you.

Need help.

With what?

Saving Irpa.

Ambitious! Good luck.

Will you help?

ME?!

No. No no no. That's not really my kinda thing.

I'm getting as far away from all this as possible.

Far away. Yes.

Look.

This place is about to go under.

Murderous demons and shadow monsters and all sorts of unsavory things I'd really like to avoid will be here in a matter of time.

But your lightning trick in Lealand bought me time to escape, so I owe you one.

Rogue's honor and all . . .

97

None of these buildings look the same. Were they all built down here?

I don't think so. That's Crogaen architecture and that's Surund.

I've seen drawings of buildings like this in Gramps's books. Those civilizations were gone even before the sun disappeared.

And what is this strange goo everywhere?

Don't touch—

—it!!

SHLURRP

SHLWARRP!!

GAH!

You were right, don't touch it!

SHWISH

What're you—?

Does it hurt?

Nah. Nope. It's fine.

Sorry about your cloak.

It's okay.

But seriously, what on Irpa **is** that stuff?

Nothing good, that's for sure.

We should keep moving.

Agreed.

A shield . . .

It's pretty.

And so light!

WHOOOSH

And nearly indestructible.

That's **Galdurian**.

No way!!

It is!

Here.
You should
have it.

No, no.
I don't **need** a shield.
It'll just mess with my
finely honed sword flow.
You keep it.

Are you
sure?

Yes! And together
we shall wield the **sword**
and **shield** of **Galduria**
as protectors of Irpa!!

Okay!

Besides, I spent
all that time learning to
blacksmith in Baihle so I could
make the world's greatest
Galdurian sword.

You **made**
your sword?

I sure did!

What the—?

What? I really did.

No, I . . . I felt like something was watching us.

I wouldn't worry. I'm pretty sure we're the only living things down here.

Yeah. You're probably right.

So . . . back to your sword . . .

How long did it take to make?

Not long. My teacher said I was the best student she ever had.

Wow.

Actually, that might not be entirely true. Maybe I drove her into early retirement. Who's to say?

But I did make this sword, and it'll never leave my side. It has seen me through many perilous situations.

Scrit Scrat

Did you hear that?

Eh?

No. I didn't hear anything.

Are you just tired of my stories?

No.

Tell me more about Baihle. How long did you live there?

Maybe ten years? It's a big place. Always a lot going on.

I didn't really like it very much.

Why not?

It was crowded but lonely. It didn't feel like home.

Hey, don't let me bring you down. **You** might love it there!

No. I just realized . . .

My home . . . It's gone. It's so far off in the dark. I can't ever go back.

I'm sorry, Bea.

It's stupid to get upset about it with everything that's happening. I just hadn't thought about it.

It's not stupid. It's important to have a home. To have somewhere you belong. I understand.

Oh, Cad. Your home. I didn't mean . . .

It's okay.

C'mon! After our stunning victory, we can find ourselves some **new** homes. Or even get our **old** ones back.

Bad things happen, and sometimes there's no explanation for them. If there's anything I've learned, it's that.

But that bird almost destroyed the entire world five hundred years ago. I might not be able to change that, but the least I can do is try and save what's left.

Cad . . .
He spoke to me.
Or showed me something.
I don't know how to describe it.

WHAT?!
You're just telling me this **now**?!

I guess I still don't really know what it was. Or how to explain it.

Try me.

He . . . looked at me.

And I was in his head. Or he was in mine . . . ? It was all a jumble. There were stars, water, plants. The sun, I think.

And feelings. Anger, pain, sadness, worry, fear. Regret. It was a lot of things, but it didn't feel **evil**.

They were all feelings **I've** felt before.

Bea, why didn't you tell me?

I don't know.

I . . . just . . .

No way!!

GRRAAAWRR!!

Back off!

SHLURRP

No!

Stop. It is ours.

You will **all** be ours.

KA-THUNK

YAH!

Did you see that?!

I'm a little preoccupied. We're going to need more water.

Over there . . . !

The door
with the fireflies.
That's where we
need to go.

SPLASH

Yes, caught. Found out. Spotted. Thrown in the dungeon.

Someone's coming— Quick!

A complete evacuation this quickly?! While the mara rushes off to chase a myth, no less.

I suppose if we must leave, we may as well leave before the masses bottleneck our harbor.

You speak more sense than the lot of them.

Sounds like trouble's on the way. We better be quick.

This will do. Get on!

This isn't your boat.

Just get in.

'EY!!! That ain't your boat!

It's not.

We'll return it. Not to worry!

THIEVES!!

We are.

It's all a matter of perspective.

Mara.

A moment, if you will.

Are you sure about this plan?

Adeline, please.

Getting the entire city onto boats?! We are unprepared for such an evacuation. We need more time.

And time is what I am going to give you.

But we also need our leader.

This city is not a fortress built for defense. We are a people of the sea. And the sea is how we will save our people.

Take the ships on our trade route—the Kilyaa River to Baihle. That's our best hope for safety.

You must lead the escape, Adeline. The people trust you. I trust you. I need you now more than ever, old friend.

Please be careful.

I'll do my best.

Okay,
I got you here.
We're even.

There.

>Huff, huff!<
Better be some
good stuff in
there.

What did
you say you
needed?

Ya know, you could
be a little more forthcoming
with information!

Well, well, well.

Ain't this something! All this stuff, just sitting here right outside the city. It's almost too good to be true!

Hey, where'd you go?

CHIK CHIK CHIK

Of course.

Ugh.
That was
a lot.

Oh no.

NIMM!

Oh no.
No no no!

I know what to do!

WHOOOSHHH

HURAK

RAOWRR

Thank goodness.

You're okay. Everything's okay.

Good as new!

That goes for you too!

How in the world did you end up down here all alone?

That must've been really scary.

We don't know where we're going, but you can come with us if you want.

SHLURP!!!

Looks like the fireflies are going that way.

Then so are we!

Would you look at that.

No.
We aren't
here to—

You doubt
the veracity
of my claim?!
Insolent
knave!

WHOOOSH

Ah, human.
To be expected.

SNIFFFFF

But this . . .
Impossible.

SNUFF

Your nose doesn't fail you.
I'm a **Galdurian**. There's a dragon
and a cat with us too.

Strange. Regardless, if you are here to slay me, you'd best get to it quickly.

I am hungry and look forward to crunching your bones.

We don't want to slay you!!

Then what could you **possibly** desire?!

We need your help.

My help?

Yes. Please.

Hm.

Before even hearing **any** request, I will require an offering.

We already left you one!

Just over there.

Do not insult me. I need a **true** offering.

≈GULP≈

155

Hm.

I know!
We will be in
your debt!

His **debt**?!
Are you sure?

Trust me.

Why would **I** ever
require **your** services?

Maybe you'll need to
get into a small space one
day to retrieve a lost object.
Or you'll be tired and will need a
strong friend to carry something.
Or you'll want somebody to
read a book aloud to you.

Call on us!

Kind of a raw deal if you ask me.

I think we're lucky he hasn't eaten us yet. But Gramps sent us here for a reason.

Lorgon must have a wealth of knowledge, even about Kest.

We could ask him to help us defeat Kest.

That's more of a request than a question.

He didn't specify.

He'll probably just say no and then we have nothing.

True. Then let's ask how to defeat Kest.

Okay.

Actually, I think we should ask who Kest **is**.

Why?

I dunno . . . something doesn't feel right.

You mean because he talked to you?

Well, yeah.

I don't see how that will help us.

Let's say Lorgon tells us how to defeat Kest, and it's something we can't do. Or he can't be defeated at all. Then what?

If we know what he is, we can figure out why he's doing this and how to stop him.

Maybe we can even find a way to undo the damage he's done and put things right.

We can make sure this never happens again.

AHEM

Your question?

That's a lot of things. Are you sure?

No, but I think it's our best chance of figuring this all out.

I created the seas faster than this!

Your call. I trust you.

Go ahead, Bea . . .

You've got this.

Who is Kest Ke Belenus?

Why do you ask this?

Uhh . . . Well, it's just . . .

You said we get to ask a question. Now if you please, answer said question.

Hm.

Kest Ke Belenus is the Spirit of Light.

Impossible!

Why do you need **my** help anyway? It was the Galdurians who stopped him the first time.

Pinned him to the ground and ripped the remaining flame from his chest, then cast him into an eternal slumber.

It was only a matter of time before he awoke. Now he has, and it's clear his opinion of the situation has not changed. He will not stop until all the flames are in his possession once more.

Not if we stop him first. And we will.

Heh. Will you now?

Yes! I will finish what my people started and rescue the light of this world from evil!

And pray tell, how do you plan on doing that?

I will destroy Kest if it's the last thing I do.

A bold claim. Careful, or it may prove to be your undoing.

But can it be done? How do we stop him?

Kill him, you mean? Oh yes, stab him in the heart, drop a boulder on him, chop off his head . . .

No special spell or magic sword or anything?

Magic sword? No, no. We Spirits can be killed. It's been done before.

If you've known Kest is awake, why haven't **you** stopped him?

Who's to say I want to?

You're a **Spirit**, for crying out loud! Don't you want to save the world?!

You and I might not have the same definition of "save," Galdurian.

I mean . . . Sorry.

You two have heart, I'll give you that.

The Waters are my only concern now, as the Lights are Kest's. We are done here.

I have answered more than one question. Kest is on his way to Rinn as we speak. I will grant you safe passage through my waters.

So much for that. Dragon, Nimm—c'mon! We're getting outta here.

They're coming. Just over the ridge.

Mara!

Thank you, Fillog. How bad does it look?

It could be worse.

Scouts!
It is time.

We have **speed** and **surprise** on our side. Stay spread out— we'll hit their flank and create chaos. Our goal is to slow them down.

Hold for my signal!

SKEEEEEE

KA KOOM

Cad, there's a light ahead!

POP

It's Rinn! We've made it!!

The Light! We're not too late.

Praise Irpa, you're alive!

Fillog!

You're wounded!

Keep still. I need to get this tight to stop the bleeding.

I'm a fool to think I could've slowed him down.

But you did! You bought your people time to escape! You saved countless lives, I'm sure of it.

They cut right through us and now our Light is lost. I have failed Rinn as its mara.

Nonsense!
The people of Lealand paid for their mara's lack of leadership. You were faced with an impossible choice. The bravery of you and your scouts saved your people.

The Light is gone, but there's still a glow in the distance.

How?

Kest must not have retrieved the Flame from within the Light yet.

This
is it.

KLANG

GYA!

SLASH

URK!

ZH-KLANG!!

218

YAHHHHH!!

SKLISHHH

I understand now. Someone special was taken from you.

I don't know who. I don't know why. But it doesn't matter. It shouldn't have happened.

My parents were taken from me before I ever knew them.

Cad not only lost his family, but **all** the Galdurians.

It feels like the world has betrayed you.

Turned its back on you.

It isn't fair. It isn't right.

And I don't know how to fix it.

But I don't think this is the way.

It can't be.

HAHAHA!! WE DID IT!!

Bea— We're heroes!!!

It doesn't feel that way.

What did you expect it to feel like?

I dunno. Better, I guess.

We saved the Flame!! Kest is defeated, destroyed once and for all!!

We've completed the Galdurian legacy. The rest of the Lights are safe. Life will go on!!!

I'm going to eat a mountain of cheese! And gorseberry pies!!

Do you think they'll give us castles? Or beach houses?

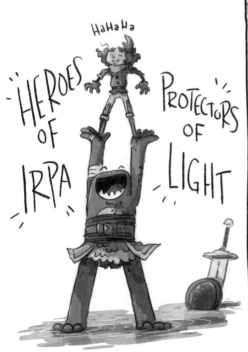
HaHaHa

HEROES OF IRPA

PROTECTORS OF LIGHT

Okay, okay. Let's get that wound wrapped up before you pass out.

Fine, but only if you promise to celebrate more after.

SPUTTER SPUTTER

?!

Look.

No!
No no no.
What's happening?!

Lucky we rescued your glowing stick, at least.

Not lucky.

Did you **know** this was going to happen?

No.

We need to get going.

Not yet.

What's that cat meowing about?

MROWR MROWR

There's something out there. In the water. Coming this way!

MROWR MROWR MROWR

They return.

Would you look at that.

MEROWRRR

What happened?

MRRRRR

We fought Kest.

And we won.

You won?! Then why is it **dark**?

The Flame was there. It was safe. And then . . .

It just faded away.

All the Lights are dark.

WHAT?! No. No, that can't be true! It can't!

It is true.

Good job.

Lorgon said this would happen.

Huh?

Lorgon.
He told us.

"One way or another, Irpa will slip back into darkness."

The Flames were part of Kest. They were a part of his very soul. He was the source of all light, and the Flames died with him.

I should've realized it before. But I didn't.

He could've just said it instead of speaking in riddles.

We could've listened. But it doesn't matter anymore.

So that's it. World's over?

Not yet.

Inspiring. What do we do now?

We should start by getting out of here. This place will be crawling with shadows soon.

Everywhere will be crawling with shadows. Where do you suggest we go?

What's **your** great idea?

I didn't cause this mess!

How 'bout I feed you to the dragon!

Better than being stuck with you!!

!!

That's it . . .

We keep going. We find the sun. We find a way to bring it back.

What?

How?

There's so much we don't know about the world.

There has to be a way.

We'll figure it out. And then we'll do it.

That's not a plan. That's just cra—

I'm with you, Bea!!

Where do we start?

I don't know.

You're all insane—

CRK

What was that?!

Something is here.

Shadows, I bet. We fight our way through. Rush them on three. Ready?

One.

Two.

?!

Beatrice?!

For Jodi

Thanks to
Mom and Dad; Bryan Probert, flatting extraordinaire;
Andrew Arnold, Rose Pleuler, Erica De Chavez,
Caitlin Lonning, Rick Farley, Anna Bernard, and everyone
at HarperAlley; Joe Burrascano, Tom Beatty, Kevin Frodell;
Kazu Kibuishi and Faith Erin Hicks.

HarperAlley is an imprint of HarperCollins Publishers.

Lightfall: Shadow of the Bird
Copyright © 2022 by Tim Probert
All rights reserved. Manufactured in Italy.
No part of this book may be used or reproduced in any manner
whatsoever without written permission except in the case of
brief quotations embodied in critical articles and reviews. For
information address HarperCollins Children's Books, a division
of HarperCollins Publishers, 195 Broadway, New York, NY 10007.
www.harperalley.com

Library of Congress Control Number: 2021948113
ISBN 978-0-06-299050-1 — ISBN 978-0-06-299048-8 (pbk.)

The artist used Prismacolor pencil, mechanical pencil, and
Photoshop to create the digital illustrations for this book.
Typography by Tim Probert and Erica De Chavez
21 22 23 24 25 RTLO 10 9 8 7 6 5 4 3 2 1
❖
First Edition